THE UGLY DUCKLING DINOSAUR

A Prehistoric Tale

BY Cheryl Bardoe ILLUSTRATED BY Doug Kennedy

ABRAMS BOOKS FOR YOUNG READERS • LONDON

Tap, tap, tap.

CRACK!

Peep, peep, peep.

nce upon a time, seven tiny beaks pecked their way out of their eggs and into a world of giant ferns, ginkgo trees, and dinosaurs. However, one egg didn't hatch. The mother duck sighed and settled onto the nest again. The next day the egg still had not hatched. A neighbour duck waddled over and quacked, "What's wrong with that egg?"

"It's extra large and slow to hatch," the mother duck said, "but I'm sure the duckling inside is as perfect as the rest."

Just then, the egg trembled.

Thump, thump, thump.

SMASH!

A huge claw burst out, followed by a gigantic foot. The newest duckling exploded from its shell.

The mother duck gasped. Her other ducklings froze and stared.

"That is the ugliest duckling I've ever seen!" the neighbour screeched.

The hatchling gazed at his siblings' dainty legs and webbed feet. He examined his own bulging thighs and sharp claws. His brothers and sisters had fluffy feathers, but he had pebbly skin. "I *am* ugly!" he cried.

"Nonsense," his mother said. "Those powerful legs will make you a fine swimmer."

Seven perfect ducklings paraded after their mother
to the swamp. One ugly duckling clomped behind.
   "There's no widdle in this one's waddle," the
neighbour duck cackled. "His teeth are too big for his
head, and his tail swooshes like a crocodile's."

The mother duck sailed into the water. Seven perfect ducklings glided behind. One ugly duckling stomped in and sloshed waves with his tail. The neighbour duck shrieked when water washed over her. "That duckling is a monster!"

Nearby, a turtle basked in the sun. "He has no feathers, either," the ugly duckling thought. "I'll go and say hello." When the duckling splashed over, the turtle retreated into its shell.

The duckling then waved to a herd of Parasaurolophuses drinking at the pond's edge. Several of the dinosaurs jerked up their crested heads. Before the water could finish dripping from their chins, the entire herd stampeded away.

The ugly duckling frowned at his reflection. Even the animals without feathers didn't have puny arms, clumsy feet, and enormous teeth and jaws like his. "I'm too ugly to fit in here," he said. "I must go find my home somewhere else in the world."

He took one last look at the sunlight glinting on the feathers of his mother and siblings. When they dove underwater, he fled into the forest.

The ugly duckling wandered day after day after day and grew and grew and grew. Soon he was so big that the ground quaked when he walked. Every animal ran from the sight of him.

Pteranodons flew away.

Lizards and small mammals hid.

Stegosauruses fled.

"I'm such a monster that no creature will look at me," the ugly duckling moaned. "I wish I was covered in feathers and that the ground didn't shake when I walked."

One day the ugly duckling spied beautiful
feathers floating on the breeze. Nearby a gathering
of Deinonychuses preened. "Aha!" the duckling said.
"If I disguise myself, perhaps they will like me."

The ugly duckling tucked feathers into the creases of his skin and under his armpits. He tiptoed into the clearing. "Hello, brothers," he said, bowing low. Oops! His feathers fluttered off.

The dinosaurs' eyes grew as big as magnolia flowers. "It's a monster! Run!"

Alone again, the ugly duckling sobbed, "I'll never find my home in the world."

BOOM! BOOM!

The ground quivered. *snap!* Branches splintered from trees. The ugly duckling heard creatures scurry through the forest, just like they usually ran from him.

"Something very ugly must be coming," he said.

A majestic dinosaur stopped before him. The bumps in the creature's skin gleamed in the sun. It had large teeth, legs as thick as palm trees, and toe claws that curved like a crescent moon. It wasn't ugly at all.

The dinosaur cocked its head. "Why are you crying, child?"

Hearing the kind words, the duckling felt the bumps on his own skin tingle. "I'm a monster. I'm such an ugly duckling that I don't belong anywhere."

"Duckling? Nonsense." The dinosaur nuzzled the little one. "Ugly? Why, you are as beautiful as my own children. Come home with me."

"Really?" The ugly duckling couldn't believe his ears. He followed the dinosaur, taking two ground-rumbling steps for every thunderous stride of hers. Soon he spied a muddy nest ahead. Youngsters stomped and played nearby with toe claws, jumbo jaws, and bulging thighs like his.

"Why, those ducklings are just like me!" said the ugly duckling.

"We are NOT ducklings. We are called Tyrannosaurus rex," said the little dinosaurs.

The mother dinosaur smiled. "Just like you."

"Just like me!" The little T. rex skipped toward the nest, proud to feel the ground tremble underfoot. And with his new family, he growled.

"HOOOOOORRRROOO- AAAARRRRRRRR!"

A duckling no more.

The following pages include scientific illustrations of the dinosaurs and other flora and fauna that play a part in this book.

Stegosaurus The bony plates poking from this dinosaur's back do not provide much defense. Rather, they may have helped these animals recognize each other and attract mates. They may also have soaked up the sun's rays to help them stay warm.

Deinonychus Feathers may have helped dinosaurs like this one to keep warm, or to attract mates—but they did not help them fly.

Parasaurolophus These dinosaurs roamed their grazing lands in huge herds.

AUTHOR'S NOTE

Scientists believe today's birds are the last branch of the dinosaur family tree. Birds evolved from theropods—the group of dinosaurs that ran on two feet. Theropods ranged from the *Tyrannosaurus rex*, which was as long as a school bus, to the turkey-sized *Velociraptor*. Birds and their closest dinosaur relatives share a lot in common. Their skeletons have more than 100 common features, including wishbones and hip sockets that hold the legs directly underneath the body. Bird eggs have the same hard shell as the eggs of dinosaurs and other reptiles. And some dinosaurs had feathers, although scientists haven't yet found a dinosaur they believe could fly.

For many years scientists thought modern birds didn't evolve until after the dinosaurs had died out. Then, in 2005, paleontologists discovered the first fossil evidence that ancient relatives of modern birds lived right alongside dinosaurs. Scientists announced that the *Vegavis iaai*, which lived more than 65 million years ago, was part of the same bird group that includes modern ducks and geese. Other fossil finds, published in 2006, showed that the *Gansus yumenensis*, which lived 110 million years ago, had webbed feet and looked like a modern waterfowl called a grebe. These fossils prove that the ancestors of modern birds shared the planet with dinosaurs and then survived whatever caused dinosaurs to go extinct.

Could a *T. rex* egg really have rolled into the wrong nest and been hatched by a *Vegavis iaai*? That seems unlikely. But who knows what may or may not have happened once upon a time, millions of years ago.

Acknowledgments

The author is grateful to Dr. Richard Kissel, at the Paleontological Research Institution and its Museum of the Earth, and to Erica Kelly, at the San Diego Natural History Museum, for sharing their expertise during the development of this book.

Vegavis iaai This reconstruction of *Vegavis iaai* (forefront) is based on a fossil found in Antarctica that was the inspiration for this book. This species was a cousin to the ancient birds that are direct ancestors of today's geese and ducks. Similar animals may have lived alongside *T. rex* in North America. (In the background is a hadrosaur, or duckbill dinosaur.)

Bibliography

Barrett, Paul. *National Geographic Dinosaurs*. Washington, DC: National Geographic Society, 2001.

BBC News. "China Fossils Fill out Bird Story." June 16, 2006.

Clark, Julia A., et al. "Definitive Fossil Evidence for the Extant Avian Radiation in the Cretaceous." *Nature*, January 20, 2005.

The Field Museum. "Evolving Planet" exhibition. Chicago, 2010.

North Carolina State University News Services. "Relatives of Living Ducks and Chickens Existed Alongside Dinosaurs More Than 65 Million Years Ago." January 19, 2005.

Suggestions for Further Reading

Kelly, Erica, and Richard Kissel. *Evolving Planet: Four Billion Years of Life on Earth*. New York: Abrams Books for Young Readers, 2008.

Kudlinski, Kathleen. *Boy, Were We Wrong About Dinosaurs!* New York: Dutton Children's Books, 2005.

Judge, Lita. *Born to Be Giants: How Baby Dinosaurs Grew to Rule the World*. Crescent City, CA: Flashpoint Press, 2010.

Zoehfeld, Kathleen Weidner. *Did Dinosaurs Have Feathers?* New York: HarperCollins Publishers, 2003.

Tyrannosaurus rex (T. rex) Huge teeth, powerful jaws, and a seven-ton body puts this meat-eater at the top of the food chain. Fossil evidence suggests that adult and young *T. rex* dinosaurs lived together in groups.

For Ethan and Amelia,
my own beautiful ducklings
—C. B.

For Julian and Jackson
—D. K.

ARTIST'S NOTE

When I was little I loved to watch the TV show *Land of the Lost* and movies like *Sinbad* because they depicted mythical creatures but also dinosaurs! When I was asked to illustrate *The Ugly Duckling Dinosaur*, I was excited because now I would be creating a land of dinosaurs for my own two sons. The first thing I did was research at my local library in Monroe, Louisiana, how the "duck" (called *Vegavis*), dinosaurs, and plants should appear. I saw many photographs of plant and dinosaur fossils, but things such as colouration and the appearance of skin and feathers are not truly known. At the library I discovered oversized books on dinosaurs with classic, beautiful reproductions of paintings of dinosaurs and their environments. However, some of the books I found—though beautifully illustrated—did not show the most recent paleontological research on how we now believe dinosaurs appeared, moved about, and lived. So I had to balance the magnificent paintings created in the early to mid part of the twentieth century with books published later incorporating the new information. The *Vegavis* is a very recent discovery, so I found a scientific painting of it online (www.livescience.com), which helped me with its appearance and imagined colouring. I want to thank Cheryl Bardoe, who shared my sketches and final artwork with scholars and other "dino" authorities to ensure my work was as accurate as possible. Taking into account, of course, that the ducks and dinosaurs were talking with one another and living out a favourite fairy tale! There had to be some poetic licence! I painted using watercolour, because many scientific illustrators use this medium, and I wanted to give my work the same feel and texture.

The Library of Congress has catalogued the hardcover edition of this book as follows:

Bardoe, Cheryl, 1971–
The ugly duckling dinosaur : a prehistoric tale / by Cheryl Bardoe ; illustrated by Doug Kennedy.
p. cm.
Includes bibliographical references (p.).
Summary: In this take on "The Ugly Duckling," a tyrannosaurus rex is hatched in a nest of ducklings. Includes facts about dinosaurs.
ISBN 978-0-8109-9739-4 (alk. paper)
[1. Tyrannosaurus rex—Fiction. 2. Dinosaurs—Fiction. 3. Ducks—Fiction.] I. Kennedy, Doug, ill. II. Title.
PZ7.B25016Ug 2011
[E]—dc22
2010021624

ISBN for this edition: 978-0-8109-9876-6

Abrams Books for Young Readers are available at special discounts when purchased in quantity for premiums and promotions as well as fundraising or educational use. Special editions can also be created to specification. For details, contact specialmarkets@abramsbooks.com or the address below.

ABRAMS
THE ART OF BOOKS SINCE 1949
72-82 Rosebery Avenue
London, UK EC1R 4RW
www.abramsbooks.co.uk

Pteranodon This species' legs pointed to the side from its hips. That's a clue that these flying reptiles were not dinosaurs. Dinosaurs' legs, such as those of the *T. rex*, point straight down from the hips.